Christmastime in Winterland

Short Stories for Families

by

Josef E. Silvia

Merry Christmas!

LuLu Independent Publishing

ISBN: 978-0-359-20195-2

Printed in the United States of America

Cover Photo by RebecaCovers via Fiverr.com

Illustrations on pages 16, 31, 34 created by Cathy Bolio. Illustrations on pages 6, 11, 23 created by Milena Vitorovic. All illustrations are copyright restricted to Cathy Bolio, Milena Vitorovic, and Josef Silvia. Photocopying of them in any form is expressly forbidden.

First Printing: November 2018

Edition A.A

Dedicated to all the children I have ever taught,
and to my sisters.

Note from the Author

Dear Friends,

The short stories you are about to read will take you to marvelous lands or remind you and your loved ones about the blessings we each receive at Christmas. It is a book not only for children, but the entire family. Almost every story locked within these pages can be read as a bedtime tale, or together before opening the presents.

It has been my aim this holiday season to create a book that families can not only enjoy but provide lessons for the parents to help teach. There is one story, *Knight Value and the Fog of Darkness,* that should only be read with a parent present as it lightly deals with a few deep themes such as self-worth. It is not a scary story, but one that may bring up important questions for you to discuss as a family.

My hope is that this little book of short stories will provide you with goodwill and be a reminder to always treasure the things we hold dear.

Happy Holidays to each of you.

Sincerely,

Josef E. Silvia

November 2018

Table of Contents

The Stories

The Illustrations

Winterland's Unicorn

Welcome to Winterland! What? You've never heard of it? Well, of course you haven't. It is a small country tucked deep away in the Artic. Not far from the North Pole, but not right next to it either. Planes, computers, or any other gizmo would never be able to find it because the people who live in Winterland use magic to make sure it is kept a secret. Who lives there? Well, Father Christmas, the Mrs., elves, reindeer, and all the unicorns do of course!

It is such a magical land! Elves work hard in a little workshop at the top of a high mountain. Winterland is always full of snow, the trees are always green and decorated, and reindeer fly around with the unicorns at will. Father Christmas and the Mrs. tend their ever-growing stable of reindeer, teaching them to fly year-round. What? You thought there were only eight? Oh, my dears, no! Father Christmas has many in his stable ready to make that yearly flight. He has to! And, sometimes, he doesn't use reindeer at all. Every so often, though none of us can ever be certain as we are all asleep when it happens, Father Christmas will ask a unicorn to help pull his sleigh by night. This happens during those busy years, when the elves are so busy making the toys that they almost don't finish in time. Or when boys and girls turn from naughty to nice rather quickly. You see, Father Christmas really doesn't enjoy giving children lumps of coal in their stocking and does his best to make sure that it hardly ever happens.

And so, Father Christmas will take out a special whistle that only the unicorns in Winterland can hear. It is shaped like a heart with red and white stripes, with a small bow at its center. When Father Christmas blows into it, a unicorn almost instantly appears before him. Each unicorn bears a striking resemblance to the other. They have light blue wings, a violet horn, and turquoise body. Their mane flows like purple drops of rain and there's always a smile within their heart. Father Christmas will be dressed in his finest green and red cloaks. His beard, dark with patches of grey and silver, is as round as the jolly face he sports. A twinkle is always in his eye, and he looks not like the department store actors but rather a simple man who loves being the surrogate father to those who remember him.

His green cap is trimmed in white and sparkles under Winterland's December Eve. Father Christmas never speaks out of turn or anger, and often the unicorn only has to look at the kind man's eyes to know what he wants. And instantly, the unicorn will hitch itself to the sleigh. "Don't stay out too late," the Mrs. will shout to her husband as he climbs into the sleigh.

Father Christmas will laugh, as he always does. And so will she, enjoying a hearty moment together. "My dear," says the kind man, "what sort of evening would it be if I wasn't out late?"

The elves wish him well and the Mrs., never one to grow used to these yearly outings, tears up as she says, "Be safe, my darling!"

The unicorn extends its wings, lifting both Father Christmas and his sleigh into the night sky. Through the years, they have had to use magic to ensure invisibility. As technology and the knowledge of people grew, Father Christmas did his best to make sure that every child—or nearly every—who celebrated this sacred Holiday would remember him and the Son of Man. Cultures changed many countries, but no matter what happened, it was always Father Christmas' aim to spread joy and peace. He always hoped that those two things would outlast every present, and perhaps throughout the entire year. As the unicorn brings him to the first stop, Father Christmas prepares himself for the landing and laughs. Happy to bless a home. Happy to spread joy. "Merry Christmas," he shouts as the unicorn brings him closer to the home. "Merry Christmas!"

Father Christmas and the Unicorn deliver gifts

The Elf who lost His Voice

There once was an elf named Evan. He, like so many other elves, wore a small blue pointed hat and golden waistcoat—the uniform to work at the workshop of Father Christmas. Evan loved the holiday season and was known to make snow angels who pour hot molasses on the snow drifts to make candy for the elf children of Winterland. Married to a wonderful lady named Tina (who was also an elf), they couldn't have children. But they had such great love. Now, Tina has a very special job in Winterland. She and only three other elves are entrusted with grooming, cleaning, and teaching the reindeer how to fly.

That's right! Tina is one of the few in the entire world who holds the secret to reindeer flying. From what we know, and this is important for this story, the reindeer eat apples that grow on trees in the coldest parts of the Winterland mountains. These apples, which are the reddest and juiciest apples you'll ever see, were found by Father Christmas centuries ago. Apparently, their seeds are from a type of tree only found in Winterland. Tina and her elves pick these apples every Christmas Eve early in the morning. They lock the apples away, pick the eight reindeer who are to fly the sleigh that night, and train them to fly. Now, I don't know what else they do besides give the reindeer apples, but from what I'm told the elves show the reindeer maps and graphs. Why? Well, the reindeer need to see what sort of things could get in their way. Like airplanes, telephone poles, and very tall buildings.

Evan often wondered what would happen if he ate one of those apples. Would he be able to fly like the reindeer? One Christmas Eve, he decided to follow his wife and her co-workers to the apple trees. He hide around the tall rocks that the Winterland mountains have many of. He didn't want to be spotted. Evan watched Tina and her friends pick the apples and then place them in a box. They locked the box once they were done and left. Looking around to make sure he was all alone, Evan tiptoed out to the apple trees. He looked up, down and all around. There wasn't an apple to be found.

"Oh, pooh!" he cried. "Pooh!"

Just then, he heard a familiar voice call his name. "Hello, Evan."

Turning around, Evan's eyes widened as Father Christmas stood before him. "Uh, hi," he stammered "Hi, Fa-father Christmas."

"What brings you out into the mountains this early in the morning?"

Evan gulped hard. "Well, I. . .uh. . . needed to find some wood for a new toy I'm building!"

"A new toy?" questioned Father Christmas.

"Yes!"

"But I thought you were working on the train sets with Charlie, Ed, and Bernie."

Evan wiped the sweat from his brow. "Well," he lied. "We finished the sets."

"All of them?" asked Father Christmas. "All three hundred?"

"Well. . ummm....no," sighed Evan.

Father Christmas shook his head. "Oh, Evan, lies are not becoming. Tina told me you might have followed her. She is worried about you, Evan."

"I'm sorry," said Evan glumly.

"I know, but you must learn your lesson. Lies are not good for you. And I won't work with an elf who lies. So, you will not be able to speak until Christmas morning."

Father Christmas snapped his fingers and Evan was suddenly back in his house. He tried to talk. No sounds came out. The next morning was Christmas Day and when it came, Evan was worried that he and Tina wouldn't be able to sing together. Every Christmas, they woke up early and went out to the village tree. They would wake up everyone around them singing joyful Christmas carols. That morning, Tina instructed him not to talk but practically had to shove him out the door. Evan was sad. He didn't mean to harm anyone. But, lies always harm someone.

Tina led Evan to the Christmas tree. Evan tried to talk, and was surprised to hear his own voice. "I knew you would," said Tina. "Father Christmas' punishments are never long but always important."

"I'm sorry, Tina," said Evan.

"I know, Evan. And I still love you."

She took his hand in hers and they looked up at the gorgeous decorated tree. "Merry Christmas!" they shouted.

And then, both Evan and Tina giggled as the bells chimed behind them and they burst into carols. "Joy to the world!"

Evan and Tina at the Christmas Tree

Knight Value and the Fog of Darkness

Many years ago in the Kingdom of Mihole lived a young knight named Value. Mihole was a beautiful Kingdom. It consisted of three main villages, Tirips, Nos, and Apap. Apap was the capitol and housed the castle as well as the large marketplace. Everything in Apap was fairly priced and no one was ever caught cheating or stealing, it was truly a wonderful place to live. Value grew up in Tirips. It was only a day's journey from Apap, smaller but still as friendly. Value's father was a nobleman of the town and had been a knight for the king when he was younger. Value grew up hearing the stories about the battles his father had fought for the king, and why he was given the name "value."

"Son," Value's father would say, "your mother and I gave you that name so you can remember how precious you are. Everyone is of value. I learned that when I served the king. He gave each of us knights special armor. And reminded us that we had value, that we are no more important than he. That when we fight in his name we are being given his authority. Because we are his."

Value married when he came of age to a woman named Eunice, and they soon had a son named Troy. Value was never so happy, until word came that he was to be a knight. It was the position he had wanted. Fortunately, being of noble birth gave him the chance to do so. But that was another interesting thing about Mihole which separated it from other countries. Most countries only allowed nobles and dukes in certain positions, and they have tremendous populations of poor. Mihole didn't. There were no poor persons in Mihole because everyone was of some sort of noble birth, either true or adopted. Years ago when Mihole was first built there were dozens of nobles and a growing number of poor who needed the basic things. The king sent his son to the poor who asked the son for help and the son simply adopted all the poor into the royal bloodline.

Value was thrilled to become a knight. He trained hard and was honored by the King when he was given his armor and sword. The armor was a staple in the Kingdom of Mihole. Every knight was fitted perfectly for their armor so that it would fit snug during battle. It was a beautiful piece to wear. And the sword Value was given, he couldn't imagine another quite like it. It was one foot high, thick and yet light as a feather. The sword also had a unique quality, it could glow at night which made it a great battle piece. For when the enemy attacked, one would never be without their sword.

About a year after he became a knight, a war ensued between the Kingdom of Mihole and the Kingdom o Wraith. The King and the Prince called all their knights to battle, and Value had to kiss his wife Eunice goodbye and his two year old son Troy. He would miss them, but the Kingdom of Wraith had to be stopped. And so, he went off to war with all the other knights. Each wearing their armor and carrying their sword. Within a few days, the war that had threatened the Kingdom of Mihole was over and all the knights returned without a scratch. The King and his Prince were so pleased that they immediately sent all their knights to return home to their loved ones.

So, Value, looking forward to seeing his wife and child again took off his armor and left it with his sword in the castle barracks and headed towards the village of Tirirps. He couldn't wait to see Eunice and Troy again. The few weeks he had spent away had felt much longer. "I love them," he whispered to himself. "So very much."

On the road home a thick, black fog crept up around Value. At first he was able to press through it but soon it had surrounded him. Before he knew it, he was in despair. He wanted to get home and doubted that he would be able to with this fog. Then he thought about the time he had spent away from his wife and child. He started criticizing himself for being away for so long. "How dare I work for the King so much," he thought. "My wife and child need me too. Maybe I have behaved foolishly and stupidly!"

While he thought these things, the fog built itself into a wall and it blocked Value's way. He tried to walk through it, but it repelled him. He saw a rock laying on the rock beside the road and picked it up, throwing hard at the fog. Unfortunately it didn't penetrate the fog at all. The rock bounced off and it Value in the head, leaving a nasty bruise. As Value rubbed the bruise, he began to cry. "I am a knight! And yet I can't even get home because of a fog! I must be worthless!"

Not knowing what else to do, Value headed back towards the castle. He asked for an audience with the Prince and was granted it almost immediately. Upon entering the Throne Room, Value told the Prince everything that was going on. Smiling, the Prince looked at Value and said to him, "My son, why didn't you wear the armor my Father the King made for you? Take the armor, and especially the sword. God back to the fog. It will protect you."

Listening to the Prince, Value did just that. He went back to the castle barracks and put his armor on. Then, he took the sword and headed back out on the road home. The fog had become an even larger wall by now, and was thicker. Value picked up another rock and hurled it at the wall, and this rock bounced almost three kilometers behind him. As the rock bounced backwards, Value had an idea. What if he lunged at the wall with the sword? Taking the sword from its sheath, Value thrust it into the blackness and was amazed to find that the sword went all the way through. He slashed at it again, and then again. Each time, the sword made tiny cuts in the wall and light had begun to shine through those cuts.

Standing back, Value had only one more idea. He would command the wall to disappear in the King's name and throw the sword at it. Taking a deep breath, he shouted, "In the King's name I command you to go!"

At the same time he said this, Value threw the sword into the center of the fog. The black wall suddenly shook and then vanished. Picking up his sword, Value put it back in its sheath and continued his journey home. He had learned an important lesson: Never be without your armor, and always carry the sword. Its truth will guide your path.

Fog coming towards Knight Value

The Christmas Flush

December 24th. It was another typical New England December in Plymouth, Massachusetts. Light patches of snow covered the ground in parts and the bare trees looked sad without their leaves or wintery covering. A small, two-story house surrounded by trees and neighbors was bustling with excitement on Wallwind Drive. Christmas was tomorrow, and Nancy Parks was busy wrapping up the many gifts strewn across her brown sofa while her husband, Jonathan, was tightening the back wheel on their twelve-year old daughter's bicycle in the safety of their bedroom. Their two children, Lucy and Devin, were busy playing with Devin's dog; a cocker spaniel named Shostakovich. Devin was two years old and had fallen in love with the little dog when his parents bought him a few months back. Everyone agreed that since the two were inseparable, Shostakovich might as well be Devin's. "All right you two," said Nancy, "time to go to bed. Brush your teeth or Santa won't come."

"But Mom," said Lucy, "there's no—"

Nancy, being a mother and schoolteacher, was accustomed to staring at children when she needed to discipline them or get them to be quiet. She had perfected a look that could make you cry if you were thirteen and haunt you if you were fifty. It was this look she gave Lucy, causing the twelve-year old girl to close her mouth almost immediately. "Um, yeah, mom, okay," said Lucy rather quietly. "C'mon, Devin, let's get ready. You first. Go use the bathroom."

"Can I try?" asked Devin.

Lucy sighed. "Yes, Devin. You'll miss. But you can try."

Nancy smiled and shook her head as her children ran up the stairs to their respective bathrooms. They had been teaching Devin to use the small toilet they purchased for toddlers but the boy simply hadn't been able to go. Nancy and Jonathan tried every trick in the book to no avail. Devin was about to be three and still in diapers. Her husband had tried to convince Devin to keep trying and if he was successful, they would buy him a brand-new fire truck for Christmas. Here it was December 24th and Devin still had not successfully used his toilet. No fire truck had been purchased, and while Devin had plenty of gifts Nancy hoped her son would be successful before the new year.

As Nancy wrapped up the presents for her sisters, cousins, and aunts Jonathan carefully walked out of the bedroom. Wiping his hands, he was gleaming. "All set, honey."

"Good!" exclaimed Nancy happily.

They had wrapped up Lucy's and Devin's gifts the night before, but the bicycle hadn't arrived until that afternoon. Jonathan spent almost four hours putting it together. "It's a lot better than the one she's had for a few years. A real keeper."

"I'm glad," said Nancy.

Just then a loud flush was heard. Then giggling followed by laughing. Nancy and Jonathan heard loud stomping on the floor above them, and a child's voice scream "Yay!!"

In a minute's time, the little feet of Devin bounded down the stairs followed by Lucy. A piece of toilet paper dangled from his right leg as he jumped up and down in his Superman pajamas. "I do it!" he screamed with glee, "I do it!"

Nancy looked up from the gifts. Her little boy was laughing, smiling, and jumping. "I do it, Mommy," he yelled, "I do it!!"

"Did what?" asked Jonathan.

"PODDY!" yelled the little boy.

Jonathan Parks gulped. He was excited, but knew what would be coming next. He asked Lucy to confirm the fact, which she did, smiling as big as her little brother. "I get the truck Daddy!" shouted Devin, "I get the truck!"

Nancy leapt to her feet chuckling as she hugged her son and Jonathan looked at his watch. It was 7 o'clock. Stores would be closing in a short two hours before the Holiday. And he had promised his little boy a fire engine for Christmas should the boy successfully use the bathroom. "I get truck, right Mommy?" asked Devin.

"We will do our best," said Nancy as she hugged Devin.

"Yay!" screamed the little boy.

"Now, go to bed, Devin. Santa will be coming real soon."

"With my truck," exclaimed the boy.

Nancy nodded as Lucy took Devin back up the stairs. The kids would soon be sleeping and they would have to bring out the gifts. But Jonathan had an errand to run. Nancy couldn't help but laugh. "Well, darling," she said, "you shouldn't have promised him a fire engine. Because now you have to get it!"

Jonathan shook his head. There was no way he would be able to find a fire engine on Christmas Eve, but he had to try. He couldn't disappoint his little boy. Throwing on his winter coat, Jonathan kissed his wife goodbye and hurried out into the cold. Most department stores were a fifteen-minute drive away, and Jonathan had to search them all before he could call it a night. Racing out Wallwind Drive and heading towards 300 Colony Place, Jonathan wasn't looking at his speedometer when he heard the sirens and saw the flashing lights. Sighing, he pulled over to the side of the road and came to a full stop. He looked at his watch, it was already thirty minutes passed the hour. Sighing, Jonathan rolled down his window as the cop approached him. "Well now, my friend," said the officer. "A bit of a speeder on Christmas Eve."

"I can explain, officer."

"Sure," replied the policeman. "Christmas shopping, or your wife is ill, I've heard them all mister. License and registration please."

Taking a deep breath, Jonathan opened his glove compartment and handed the officer his license along with the registration. "Well, Mister Parks," said the policeman, "this little Christmas drive is going to cost you three bucks."

Blinking, Jonathan couldn't help but look stunned. "Three dollars?" he inquired.

"Yes," said the officer returning Jonathan's belongings along with a ticket. "Payable after the Holiday. Merry Christmas. And don't let me see you speed down these roads again."

"No sir," said Jonathan with a smile. "Thank you, sir. Merry Christmas!"

As the cop walked back to his car, Jonathan kept an eye on his speedometer until he reached Box Mart, parking as close to the entrance as possible. Hurrying into the store, he bumped into a sales clerk accidentally. "My apologies," said Jonathan.

The salesman nodded. "Yeah. I know. Toys are in the back."

"Thank you."

"And we close in an hour," said the salesman.

"I won't need it, but thank you," said Jonathan.

Racing to the back of the store, Jonathan joined the hoards of other moms and dad as they walked around the toy section. Looking in every aisle, Jonathan finally came to the toddler toys. Most of the large trains and cars had already been taken. But a bright red fire engine sat in a lonesome corner. It was almost calling to Jonathan. Bending down, he put his hand on the truck. At the same moment, another hand touched his and he looked up. A woman with disheveled hair and a long green winter coat stared at him. They both eyed each other for what felt like minutes but was truly only seconds. Breathing heavily, the woman picked up her hand. "You saw it first," she said. "Merry Christmas."

"Thank you," nodded Jonathan with a smile. "Merry Christmas."

Picking up the toy, Jonathan made his way to the register counters. Another long line greeted him, but he did not care. His little boy was not going to be disappointed. And while Jonathan promised himself he would never make a rash promise again, he couldn't help but smile. Devin was going to have a great Christmas, Jonathan was making sure of it. Especially after the Christmas flush.

Devin and his fire engine on Christmas Day

The Christmas Princess

Did you know that there are princes and princesses living in America? I'll bet you didn't. Many of them go unnoticed by the general public. No, these princes and princesses are not of royal blood. We don't have true royalty here in America. But, the princes and princesses of America deserve their titles. Why? Because of their actions and who they are on the inside. There is a lot more to being a princess or prince than just having a Mommy and Daddy who are the King and Queen. And I want to introduce you to one of these princesses: Jodi Fletcher.

Jodi was five years old three Christmases ago when her loving Mommy passed away in the middle of the night. Something was wrong with her heart and Jodi tried to understand it when her Daddy told her what happened. "See, Jodi," he said, "sometimes God loves Mommies so much that he can't wait to bring them to Heaven. Your Mommy loved you very much but she didn't have a healthy heart. We knew it could cause her pain one day. We just didn't know when."

Crying, Jodi hugged her Daddy. She was going to miss her Mommy so very much. When she started first grade the year later, a lot of kids talked about their Mommies and Daddies. But Jodi didn't know what to talk about. Her Mommy was gone and her Daddy was very sad. He would leave the house without shaving, and sometimes his boss would call him at home and yell at him over the phone. Jodi heard some of these conversations when she was at the dinner table. Daddy's boss always seemed to call them when they were eating.

Jodi decided that when Christmas came, she would give her Daddy the best gift she could. A small bracelet that she would make him to wear, so he could always remember she loved him. Even when work got mean and bosses got mad. Grandma helped little Jodi wrap up the bracelet and on Christmas morning she was so very excited! Jodi handed her Daddy the gift. "What's this?" he asked.

"Open it, Daddy," she exclaimed. "Please!"

Her Daddy did and held up a beautiful hand-made purple bracelet. "It's for you to wear, Daddy. To always remember I love you. I know your boss can be mean. But I love you."

Jodi's Daddy hugged her. "Thank you, honey," he said. "You are my princess. My Christmas princess."

Jodi gives the present to her Dad.

The Prayer of Father Christmas

On every December 24th, as Father Christmas flies through the night sky, he prays a blessing on each child throughout the world; whether they celebrate the Holiday or not. Now, I can't tell you where I got a copy of this special blessing, for that is a secret. But, I am allowed to share it with you. I hope it fills you with joy and reminds you that there are always people looking over you. Especially Father Christmas.

THE BLESSING

A blessing I give you with each gift I bring

A prayer from my heart to yours.

For those who celebrate this sacred Holiday, and for those who do not.

Our Creator doesn't overlook anyone;

And neither do I.

I pray that you, dear children, will grow in wisdom, virtue, and kindness.

Wisdom for learning.

Virtue for understanding.

Kindness for all.

May each of you remember your blessings.

The big and small ones.

From your friends to your families.

And all those who stand guard over you.

And as I pray for you, dear children, I ask you pray for us.

For every Mommy, Daddy, Big Brother, Big Sister;

we need your prayers.

We don't see the world like you.

We can get angry, hurtful, and forget our common humanity.

Please, dear children, pray for us.

And with you, I pray for peace.

A peace for your families.

Your homes.

Your loved ones.

And our world.

May each of you carry the peace and blessings of this Holiday

Day by day

Year by Year

And, my dear children, may your futures be blessed.

Merry Christmas, little ones.

Never forget you are cared for.

Merry Christmas.

St. Nick prays for me and you each Christmas

About the Author

Josef Silvia was born in Leominster, Massachusetts and raised in a military family until his father became a minister in the early 1990s. During his childhood, Josef enjoyed writing stories and would often retell classic fairytales to his classmates and friends. Many people encouraged him, including his fifth through sixth grade teachers. They helped Josef discover how to construct a story from beginning to end and how to truly enjoy writing. When he was in Middle School, Josef wrote his first novella.

Apart from writing stories, Josef had always been an avid member of multiple theater groups. He apprenticed at The Priscilla Beach Theater school of acting between 2000-2005, learning how to act and write for the stage. Between 2010 and 2014, Josef wrote many adaptations of public domain fairytales for children's theater. He was also a children's pastor for over 10 years.

Having written a trilogy of novels for young adults in the Mystic Forest Series, Josef wanted to get back to his roots and focus on a book for children and families. The happy result was *Christmastime in Winterland.*

Other Books by the Author

The Mystic Forest Series:

SNOW: Journey Through the Mystic Forest

A young adult novel and retelling of the classic Snow White tale. Helseba is the evil witch of Faerydale. She wants to be the most powerful creature in all the land, but first needs the heart of someone more powerful than her; Snow.

ISAAC: A Wishing Stone in the Mystic Forest

A young adult novel and follow-up to SNOW. Helseba returns to reclaim her throne. The humans want to take control of all the magic, but first must be in possession of a wishing stone. A story about love, compassion, and an allegory on life's decisions, this book will keep you on the edge of your seat!

FAERYDALE: Before the Mystic Forest

A young adult novel and final book in the Mystic Forest Series. Set hundreds of years before the previous two, you will meet new characters and discover how all the legends began!

MERRY CHRISTMAS